T0197464

TRUMP'S LESSONS FOR KINTERGARDEN

HOW TO SURVIVE SCHOOL THE BEST

WRITTEN BY

James R. Senicola

AuthorHouse™
1663 Liberty Drive
Bloomington, IN 47403
www.authorhouse.com
Phone: 1 (833) 262−8899

This book is printed on acid−free paper.

ISBN: 978−1−7283−7119−1 (sc)
ISBN: 978−1−7283−7118−4 (e)

Library of Congress Control Number: 2020915921

Print information available on the last page.

Published by AuthorHouse 09/04/2020

authorHOUSE®

FOREWORD

I, LITTLE DONNIE, KINDERGARTEN PRESIDENT, WOULD LIKE TO CONGRATULATE YOU ON BEING ALMOST THE SMARTEST PERSON EVER (AFTER ME OF COURSE) FOR BUYING THIS BOOK. THIS IS THE GREATEST BOOK YOU WILL EVER READ BECAUSE THIS IS THE GREATEST BOOK EVER RITEN. ITS SAD THAT YOU READ BOOKS (LAME) BUT AT LEAST ITS THIS ONE YOUR READING. I AM THE BEST RIGHTER I HAVE THE BEST WORDS AND I AM THE BEST KINDERGARDENER THAT THERE EVER WAS AND WANT TO MAKE YOU BE GOOD BUT NOT AS GOODER THAN ME IN SKOOL . THAT MEANS I KNOW HOW TO RITE A BOOK AND SO I ROTE THIS WON FOR YOU. I DIDN'T GET HELP FROM ANYONE NO MATTER WHAT THE FAKE SCHOOL NEWSLEDDER SAYS, AND I DEFINITLY DID NOT PICK MY NOSE LAST WEEK. ANYWAY ENJOY THE GREATEST BOOK YOU WILL EVER READ...EVER RITTEN...IN THE WORLD...OF ALL TIME...IN ALL THE UNIDED STATES...AND SPACE...MARS 2...MAYBE HEAVEN...

LESSON 1: RIDING THE BUS

DON'T RIDE THE BUS. BUSSES ARE BIG AND SMELLYLY AND FILLED WITH LOTS OF BAD HOMBRES AND NASTY GIRLS. IF YOU'RE SMART YOU'LL DO WHAT I DO AND HAVE YOUR PERSONAL SHOWFUR TAKE YOU. I DON'T KNOW WHY EVERYONE DOESN'T JUST DO THAT?

LESSON 2: DEALING WITH LIB TEACHERS

WE ALL KNOW THAT ALL TEACHERS ARE CRY BABY DEMORCRATES. THEY ALWAYS SAY THINGS LIKE SHARE, KEEP YOUR HANDS TO YOURSELF, IF YOU HAVE NOTHING NICE TO SAY DON'T SAY IT. THAT'S STUPID AND THERE STUPID. WHEN YOU WALK IN TELL THEM YOU ALREADY KNOW EVERYTHING THEY ARE GONNA TEACH YOU BECAUSE YOUR BRAIN IS HUGE AND ITS FILLED WITH GOOD STUFF. . . THE BEST STUFF. IF ALL ELSE FAILS TELL THEM "YOUR FIRED!"

LESSON 3: DEALING WITH BULLIES

I DON'T KNOW HOW TO HELP YOU HERE. I HAVE NEVER MET A BULLY. STUPID NASTY NANCY SAYS ME AND MY BUDDY VLAD ARE BULLIES. I'M NOT SO I PROVED IT TO HER BY FAKING A HIGH FIVE, RIPPING HER STUPID SCARF AND CALLING HER NERVOUS NANCY. NO ONE CALLS ME BULLY AND GETS AWAY WITH IT. VLAD WAS SO FUNNY. HE WENT UP TO YUKI AND JUST TOOK HIS DESK AWAY FROM HIM. IT WAS SO FUNNY...HOW CAN PEOPLE CALL US BULLIES? WERE HEROS AND SUPER FUNNY!

LESSON 4: THE NURSES OFFICE AND WHY ITS OVER-RATED

I DON'T GO TO THE NURSES OFFICE VERY OFTEN BECAUSE I AM THE HEALTHIST KINDERGARDENER. IT'S A WEIRD PLACE, THE NURSES ARE ALWAYS WEARING SILLY MASKS OVER THERE NOS AND MOUF. THEY SAY IT PROTECTS EVERYONE. IM NOT BUYING IT. LAST WEEK THERE WAS A LICE OUTBREAK THAT WAS COMPLETELY OVERATED AND PROBABLY CAME FROM THE JACKIE CHAN KID. THE NURSES SAID THEY NEEDED TO TEST EVERYONE AND GET THEM HELP. WHY DO YOU HAVE TO TEST EVERYONE? IF YOU TEST LESS PEOPLE THERE WILL BE LESS CASES. LESS CASES MEANS LESS LICE. IF YOU DO HAVE LICE DON'T STAY HOME JUST WEAR A BASEBALL HAT OR SHAVE YOUR HEAD. SIMPLE. I MEAN ITS NOT LIKE LICE SPREADS.

LESSON 5: MAKE SPELLING GREAT AGAIN

AS YOU CAN TELL FROM READING THIS BOOK IM GREAT AT WORDS AND STUFF. SOMETIMES I MAKE WORDS UP THAT EVERYBODY LOVES. THE FAKE SCHOOL MEDIA MAKES ME SAD. THEY SAY I DON'T KNOW HOW TO SPELL BUT THEY COULDN'T BE MORE RONG. I EVEN DO THE TOUGH 4TH GRADE WORDS, LIKE COVFEFE. THE PRINCIPLE SAYS ITS NOT A WORD BUT HE IS A LIAR... HE DRINKS THAT STUFF EVERYDAY!

SMOCKING GUN
PRINC
WHALES
HAMBERDERS
COVFEFE
MELANIƎ
HUSTORY
TƎXT MASSAGES
KICK
MƎ

LESSON 6: DOMINATING THE LUNCHROOM

THE LUNCHROOM IS NOT JUST A PLACE TO EAT TASTY HAMBERDERS AND FRIES. ITS WHERE YOU CAN MAKE FRENDS. EVERYONE WANTS TO BE MY FIREND I HAVE SO MANY FRENDS. MY BEST FRIENDS ARE VLADY P, KIMIE J, MIKEY P... AND ...UHHHHHHHHHHHHH... UMMMMMMMM... AND SO MANY MORE. TOO MANY TO NAME. I LET THAT FOURANER BAROCKO HAVE A FEW.

LESSON 7: PLAY TIME

PLAY TIME IS A CHANCE TO PAY ATENSION ON THE THINGS YOU LIKE. I LIKE TO USE THE BLOX. I BILD KOOL THINGS LIKE WALLS AND CASINOS. I USE WALLS TO STOP PEOPLE FROM COMING INTO MY PLAY SPACE. IT TOTALLY WORKS. I NEED MORE BLOX. I TOLD VICE PRINCIPLE NEITO HE NEEDED TO SUPPLY THE BLOX. HE SAID NO, AND I SAID YOU'LL PAY FOR THIS. I JUST ENEDED UP BRINGING MY OWN.

LESSON 8: NAP TIME SCHMAP TIME

NAP TIME IS THE BEST TIME, BUT NOT IF YOU USE IT TO NAP. SLEEP IS FOR THE WEAK. I USE MY NAP TIME TO CHECK UP ON ALL THE IMPORTANT NEWS GOING ON. ONCE THE TEACHER TOOK MY PHONE. I HAVE THE BEST BRAIN SO I USED IT TO CONVINCE HER TO RETURN IT IN SECONDS NOW THAT'S THE ART OF THE DEAL.

LESSON 9: HISTORY. THOSE WHO DON'T LEARN IT ARE DESTINED... TO NOT NO IT VERY GOOD!

I WILL BE THE FIRST TO ADMINT THAT I DON'T REALLY LIKE HISTORY. THE TEACHER ALWAYS TALKS ABOUT THESE GREAT MEN WHO DID BAD THINGS. THESE MEN DID A LOT OF GOOD THINGS, GREAT THINGS, AMAZING THINGS. THINGS THAT ARE BIGGER THAN THE BAD. STALIN? WELL ORGANIZED, GREAT MUSTACHE. SADAM? SOLID COMMANDER, AWESOME MUSTACHE. VLAD THE IMPALER? GREAT NAME, GREAT MUSTACHE. CHARLIE CHAPLIN? SAVED GERMENY FROM THE GREAT DEPRESSION, GREAT MUSTACHE.

LESSON 10: GYM CLASS AND HOW TO MAKE YOUR BODY AS SEXY AS MY BODY

I AM ALWAYS THE BEST ATHLETE. THERE ARE NOT MANY SPORTS PEOPLE WHO ARE BETTER THAN ME. I DON'T PLAY THE SAVAGE SPORTS (FOOTBALL, BASKETBALL, BASEBALL ALL FOR DUMMIES.) THEY ARE TOO EASY! REAL SPORTS LIKE TENNIS AND GOLF ARE FOR PEOPLE LIKE ME WITH PERFECT BODIES.

LESSON 11: CLASS PETS AND HOW TO CARE FOR THEM

DOGS? STUPID. HAMSTERS? WHO AM I, A HOLLYWOOD ACTOR?. FISH? LAME.

THE BEST CLASS PET IS A PUSSYCAT. WHY? BECAUSE THEY ARE GREAT! THEY DO WHATEVER I SAY AND YOU CAN GRAB PUSSIES WHENEVER YOU WANT, BUT MAKE SURE YOU GRAB THEM FAST. THEY WONT LIKE IT, BUT WHO CARES? SOMETIMES YOU CAN GET IN TROUBLE WHEN YOU JUST GRAB THEM, BUT YOU CAN LIE AND SAY YOU DIDN'T. WHO ARE THE ADULTS GONNA BELIEVE? YOU OR THE PUSSY?

LESSON 12: SHARING IS NOT CARING.

ONE OF THE BIG THINGS WE ARE TAUGHT IN SCHOOL IS TO SHARE. DON'T!!!! HOW CAN I MAKE KINTERGARDEN GREAT AGAIN IF I AM ALWAYS SHARING MY STUFF? PENCILS, CRAYONS, GLUE, TAXES.... WHERE DOES IT END? IF I SHARE MY STUFF, THEY WILL NEVER LEARN HOW TO ASK THEIR DAD TO GET THEM MORE STUFF. NOW I WILL MAKE A DEAL WITH THEM FOR MY STUFF. I AM THE GREATEST DEAL MAKER.

LESSON 13: DOING MATH GOOD

REMEMBER NUMBERS ARE EASY CAUSE YOU CAN MAKE THEM WHATEVER YOU WANT. LET ME SHOW YOU. IF 4 PEOPLE COME TO MY SHOW & TELL AND THAN 6 PEOPLE ARE ALREADY THERE, HOW MANY PEOPLE CAME TO MY SHOW & TELL?

EASY! 1 MILLION!!

LESSON 14: SCIENCE IS FAKE NEWS

MOST SCIENCE IS JUNK. ITS NOT TRUE.

GLOBAL WARNING – JUNK SCIENCE. IT SNOWED LAST YEAR SO WHAT ARE THEY TALKING ABOUT? ALSO I SEE A LOT OF GREEN HOUSES ON MY BLOCK AND NONE OF THEM LOOK LIKE THEY ARE PASSING GAS, HOW WOULD A HOUSE PASS GASS?

LAST WEEK WE LEARNED ABOUT DIFFERENT KINDS OF ENERGY. ITS ALL LIES. THE SUN IS LIKE 1000 MILES AWAY. HOW CAN IT GIVE US ENERGY? WINDMILLS GIVE YOU CANCER NOT ENERGY. NOW COAL, THAT MAKES ENERGY … AND DIMONDS. NATURAL GAS? EVEN BETTER! MY FAMILY CAN MAKE THAT FOR FREE, ESPISHALLY ON TACO BOWL NIGHT AT MAR–A–LARGO.

LESSON 15: RIGHTING: THE TWEET IS MIGHTER THAN THE PEN

BY FAR MY FAVORITE SUBJECT. RITTING IS LIKE TALKING BUT WITH WORDS, AND WE ALL KNOW HOW GOOD I AM AT WORDS. THE TEACHER WANTS US TO PRATICE RITING A LOT, BUT I SAY HEY WHY RITE SENTENCES WHEN I CAN SAY THE SAME THING IN 160 LETTERS. MY SCHOOL WORK IS GOOD. (I ALWAYS GET F'S WHICH MEENS FANTASTIC) BUT I DO MY BEST WORK AT HOME OR IN SCHOOL... WHILE I AM IN THE BAFROOM...ON THE POTTY. I'LL GIVE YOU A XAMPL:

NOW THE TEACHER IS TRYING TO TELL MY PARENTS THAT I WANTEED A MOTE STUFFED WITH ALLEYGATORS AND SNAKES, WITH A SPARKING FENCE AND SHARP SPIKES ON TOP AT THE PLAYGROUND BOARDER. I MAY BE TOUGH ON PLAYGROUND SECURITY, BUT NOT THAT TOUGH. THE TEACHER HAS GONE CRAZY. #FAKENEWS

BONUS LESSON: CAREER DAY

WHEN YOUR IN KINTERGARDEN, YOU'LL BE INTRODUCED TO ALL TYPES OF CAREERS FOR WHEN YOU'RE AN ADULT. ONE DAY, WE GOT TO MEET A POLICE OCCIFER, A FIREMAN, A DOCTER, A LIBERIAN, AND EVEN A ANIMAL DOCTER. LAME!!!! UNFORTUNATELY, WE COULDN'T MEET ANY BUSINESS GUYS IN SOOTS OR THE PRESIDENT BECAUSE HE WAS "TOO BUSY..." THAT'S THE ONE I WANTED TO MEET THE MOST BECAUSE WHEN MY TEACHED ASEKD ME WHAT I WANT TO BE WHEN I GROW UP, I TOLD HER THE PRESIDENT OF THE UNIDED STATES OF AMRICA. WHEN SHE ASKED ME WHY, I TOLD HER THAT THE ANSWER WAS EASY. I'D BE GREAT AT IT! YOU HAVE TONS OF PEOPLE WORKING FOR YOU ALL OF THE TIME. MOST IMPORTANTLY, YOU GET TO LIVE IN A HUGE WHITE HOUSE, WHICH IS MY FAVORITE COLOR. EVERYONE KNOWS WHITE IS THE SUPERIOR COLOR!

MY FINAL THOTS

AS THE PRESIDENT OF KINDAREGARDEN, I HAVE HAD TO FIGHT A LOT OF LOSERS WHO ARE HATERS AND DUMMY HEADS. I SURVIVED AND WENT ON TO BECOME THE GREATEST PRESIDENT THE SCHOOL HAS EVER SEEN. I HOPE THAT AS YOU READ THIS IT WILL ENCOURAGE YOU TO YOU TRY AND BE AS GREAT AS ME. IF YOU LEARN ANYTHING FROM THIS BOOK REMBER THIS. IF YOU ARE GONNA BE GREAT AT ANYTHING, BE GREAT AT EVERYTHING. BE GREAT AT WORDS, BE GREAT AT SPORTS, BE GREAT AT PLAYGROUNDS, BE GREAT AT EATTING, BE GREAT AT LYING, BE GREAT AT NAPS, BE GREAT AT RITING, BE GREAT AT BEING GREAT. IF YOU CAN DO THAT AS GREAT AS ME THAN YOU WILL BE GREAT LIKE ME BUT NEVER GREATER THAN ME SO DON'T TRI BEING THAT GREAT BECAUSE YOU CAN NEVER BE GREATER THAN THE GREAT DONNIE T. YOUR WELCOME FOR THIS GREAT BOOK. HAVE A GREAT DAY. REMEMBER TO VOTE FOR ME NEXT YEAR AND MAKE 1ST GRADE GREAT AGAIN.

THE END?

THE LAME AUTHOR WANTED ME TO MAKE
SURE I PUT IN HIS DEDICATIONS.

HE DIDICATES THIS BOOK FIRST TO HIS MOM, ANNETTE.
HE SAYS HIS MOM'S HATE FOR ME IS ONLY EQUAL
TO HER LOVE AND SUPPORT FOR HER SON. (SHAME
WE ALL NO SHE LOVES ME. EVERYONE DOES) HE
SAYS HE WANTS TO THANK HIS DAD, JIM AND HIS
SISTER CARA FOR THERE CONSTISTINT SUPPORT.
(NO CLUE WHY ANYONE THANKS THERE FAMILY. MY
FAMILY NEVER HELPED ME WITH ANYTHING EVER).

"A SPECIAL THANKS TO NIKKI WHO HAS BEEN A
CONSTANT CHEERLEADER FROM THE START TO END
OF THIS BOOK, (SORRY SHE CHEERS FOR A LOSING
TEAM INSTEAD OF TEAM MKGA.) HIS UNCLE PETER
WHO HELPED HIM START THIS PUBLISHING JOURNEY

(I HEAR HE IS A LIB COLLEGE PROFESSOR, SAD)
AND HIS FRIEND AND ILLUSTRATION SUPPORT LAURA
(WHO HELPED DRAW MY GIANT HANDS 2 SMALL)

Printed in the United States
By Bookmasters